WITHDRAWN

P9-CDH-066

EX LIBRIS

UNIVERSITATIS SANCTI JOANNIS

The
PORCUPINE MOUSE

by Bonnie Pryor   pictures by Maryjane Begin

Morrow Junior Books · New York

LibSc
PZ
7
P94965
Po
1988

Text copyright © 1988 by Bonnie Pryor
Illustrations copyright © 1988 by Maryjane Begin
All rights reserved.
No part of this book may be reproduced or utilized in any form or by any means,
electronic or mechanical, including photocopying, recording or by any information storage and retrieval system,
without permission in writing from the Publisher.
Inquiries should be addressed to
William Morrow and Company, Inc.,
105 Madison Avenue,
New York, NY 10016.
Printed in the United States of America.
1 2 3 4 5 6 7 8 9 10
Library of Congress Cataloging-in-Publication Data
Pryor, Bonnie.
The porcupine mouse.
Summary: Two mouse brothers find it difficult to live together
until a cat threatens to do away with one of them.
[1. Mice—Fiction.   2. Brothers—Fiction]   I. Begin, Maryjane, ill.   II. Title.
PZ7.P94965Po   1988   [E]   87-12216
ISBN 0-688-07153-8
ISBN 0-688-07154-6 (lib. bdg.)

To Bob, who protects us from cats and owls—B.P.

To my mother and Clem—M.B.

Mama Mouse's house was very crowded. She couldn't even sweep the floor without tripping over one of her mouse children. There were children on the chairs. There were children behind the chairs. There were children on the beds and under the beds. Children were in the bathtub, and more were in the kitchen sink. One day, there was even a child hanging from the chandelier.

"Louie and Dan," said Mama Mouse, "you two are the oldest. It is time for you to go out into the world and find a house of your own."

So Louie and Dan packed all their belongings in a bag and kissed their mother good-bye. "Remember," said Mama Mouse, "always eat a good breakfast. Keep a clean handkerchief in your pocket. And never forget that the world is full of cats and owls."

"We will remember," promised the brothers. They waved good-bye and set off down the road to find a house.

"What if night comes and we haven't found a house?" Louie trembled. "Maybe a cat will find us, or even an owl."

"Don't worry," Dan boasted. "I am not afraid of any old cat or owl. If one comes near me, I will just poke him in the nose and scare him away."

The brothers walked and walked, but when evening came, they still had not found a perfect house. Louie listened to the wind whispering through the trees. He saw the shadows dancing on the ground. Louie shivered and walked close to Dan.

"I'm sure we'll find a house very soon," said Dan. His voice sounded brave, but he was shivering, too.

All of a sudden a shadow swooped down from a tree. "It's an owl!" yelled Dan.

He ran to hide under an old maple tree and fell right through a door hidden under the roots. Louie tumbled in behind.

Louie peeked out. He saw a leaf float by and land on the ground. "It wasn't an owl after all," he told Dan.

Dan's face turned very red. "I knew it all the time," he said crossly. "I was only playing a trick. And besides, I wanted to show you this wonderful house I found."

Louie and Dan looked all around the little house. "It's perfect," said Louie.
"Of course," Dan said smugly. "But I am tired. Tomorrow we will decorate
our house. Right now I am going to sleep."

Louie put on his pajamas. He washed his face and brushed his teeth. At last he climbed into bed, but Louie could not sleep.

"Dan, are you awake?" he called.

Dan did not answer.

"Dan," called Louie even louder, "are you awake?"

Dan opened one eye. "No," he said. "I am asleep."

"But Dan," said Louie, "how can you be asleep? You have one eye open."

Dan sat up in bed. "I guess you are right. I am awake."

"Good," said Louie. "I can't sleep without a bedtime story. Mama Mouse always told us a bedtime story."

Dan thought and thought. "I don't know any bedtime stories," he said at last. "I am too tired." He pulled up the covers and closed his eyes.

Louie tried to go to sleep. But he thought about cats with green shining eyes.
He thought about owls swooping down from the trees.

"Dan," he called, "are you awake?"

Dan kept both eyes closed.

I know, said Louie to himself, I will sing myself a bedtime song. He sat up in
bed and sang.

> *It is sad to be a mouse,*
> *Alone in a brand-new house.*
> *Thinking about cats and owls . . .*

"Dan," called Louie, "what rhymes with owls?"

Dan sat up in bed. "Towels," he said, looking very grouchy. "Now go to sleep."

"But Dan," Louie said softly, "towels doesn't fit."

"It is very late!" shouted Dan. "I am trying to sleep. Please go to bed."

"I can't sleep without a bedtime story," said Louie sadly.

"Then tell yourself a story," Dan said.

"That's a wonderful idea," said Louie. "Once upon a time there were two little mice. They were brothers, and they were best friends. One day they left their home to find a house of their own. . . ."

"Go on," said Dan. "Now I am wide-awake. I want to hear the rest of the story."

But Louie didn't answer because he was fast asleep.

The next morning Louie woke up very early. I will make breakfast for Dan, he thought. It will be a nice surprise.

He hurried to Mr. Rat's store and bought some lettuce and peas, and some cracker crumbs. When Louie got home, he woke up Dan.

"I want cookies for breakfast," said Dan.

"Mama Mouse told us always to eat a good breakfast," Louie reminded him.

"Mama Mouse is not here," said Dan. "In our house we can have whatever we want. And I want cookies for breakfast every day."

Louie went back to Mr. Rat's store. This time he bought butter and eggs, and flour and sugar. He went home and baked a big batch of cookies.

"These are delicious," said Dan. He ate a cookie, and so did Louie. Then they both had another and another, until at last the cookies were gone.

Louie's face looked a little green. "I don't feel very well," he said.

"Neither do I," said Dan. "I'll bet we are catching a cold."

"Shall I make cookies for breakfast tomorrow?" asked Louie.

"No," said Dan. "I've decided that cookies every day would be boring. Tomorrow let's have some lettuce and pea soup like Mama Mouse always makes."

Dan put on his sneakers. "This house is too plain. I am going to find things to make it look beautiful." He went out and slammed the door before Louie could say a word.

Louie looked around. Dan hadn't made his bed and his pajamas were on the floor. All the cookie dishes were waiting to be washed.

Dan is a very messy mouse, grumbled Louie to himself. He went right to work. He washed the dishes and made the beds. Then he mopped the floor and dusted the furniture. He even hung a picture of Mama Mouse over the chair.

Dan will be surprised when he sees how hard I've worked, thought Louie. He will probably feel sorry he didn't stay and help.

Just then Dan came home. He dumped a bagful of things right in the middle of the clean floor.

"Stop," cried Louie. "Can't you see I just cleaned the floor?"

"But look what I found," said Dan. "Here are some lovely pebbles to put on the table, and pinecones for the shelf. And this blue marble will look terrific by our beds."

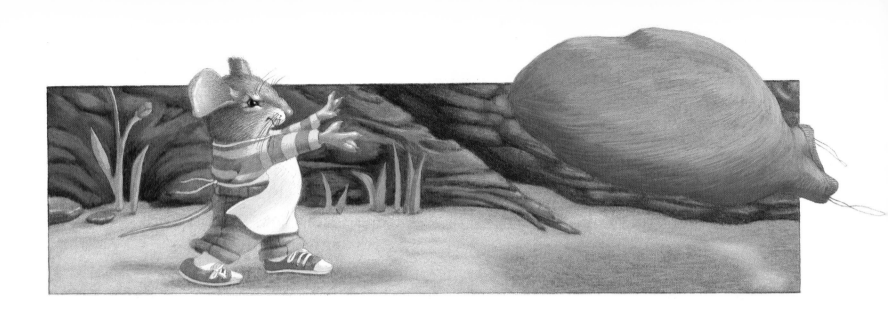

"I don't want dirty old rocks on the table," said Louie. "And I certainly don't want pinecones on the shelf. I don't even want a marble by our beds." He threw everything back in the sack, pricking his finger on the tip of a pinecone. That made him even crosser. He tossed the bag out the door.

"I worked all day to find those things," shouted Dan.

"I worked all day to clean the house," said Louie.

The two brothers glared at each other. By bedtime they weren't even speaking.

Bump!

"What was that?" asked Louie. He hid under his covers.

Dan jumped out of bed. "I think someone is stealing my beautiful things. I'm going to go out and get them, and bring them into the house."

"Oh, Dan," said Louie, shaking under the covers, "what if there is a cat out there?"

"Don't be silly," said Dan.

He opened the door and peeped outside. It was very dark and there were strange black shadows. Dan wished he was back in his bed, snug and safe. But he did not want Louie to think he was afraid. He took a deep breath and ran out to grab the sack. When he picked it up, he saw two green eyes staring at him.

"Hello," purred the cat. "You look like a lovely snack."

Louie was watching out the window. He saw the shiny eyes and sharp teeth. "Oh, dear," he cried. "The cat will gobble up Dan, and it's all my fault. Why did I throw that bag outside?"

Then Louie had an idea. He opened the door just a little.

"Yum, yum," said the cat. "Another midnight snack."

"Would you like some medicine for your tummyache?" asked Louie, trying to sound brave.

"I don't have a tummyache," said the cat.

"Not yet," said Louie. "But you will have one after you eat Dan."

"Why would a mouse snack give me a tummyache?" asked the cat.

"You think that Dan is a mouse?" Louie chuckled. "That is a good joke. Anyone can see that Dan is really a porcupine."

"Ho," said the cat. "I know all about porcupines. They have quills that poke, and they are very bad to eat. I don't see any quills on this fellow."

"I see you don't know very much about porcupines," Louie answered quickly. "At night we take off our quills and put them in a sack. Reach in the sack if you don't believe me."

The cat stretched his paw very carefully into the sack. But he touched the end of a prickly pinecone. "Ouch!" yelled the cat, licking his paw. "I almost made a terrible mistake. I will never come back here again." The cat ran away very fast.

Dan raced into the house and locked the door. "Louie," he cried, "you saved my life. I didn't know you were so brave."

Louie sat down in a chair. "I didn't know I was so brave, either," he said in a tiny voice. "From now on, you can be the brave one. Being brave makes my knees shake."

Dan made them both a cup of tea. They sat by the fire and looked at Dan's beautiful things. Soon Louie's knees stopped shaking.

"I have a new song," said Louie. He sang the song to Dan.

It is good to be a mouse,
In a cozy little house.
Right by the fire I sit,
And cats and owls don't scare me a bit.
"That's a good song," said Dan.
Louie and Dan closed their eyes.
Soon they were both sound asleep.

LibSc PZ 7 .P94965 Po 1988
Pryor, Bonnie.
THe porcupine mouse

WITHDRAWN